T0142722

EVER SINCE
I WAS
7 SEVEN

Based on a true story

authorHOUSE

AuthorHouse™
1663 Liberty Drive
Bloomington, IN 47403
www.authorhouse.com
Phone: 833-262-8899

Published by AuthorHouse 02/09/2022

ISBN: 978-1-6655-5013-0 (sc)
ISBN: 978-1-6655-5012-3 (e)

...this book is for everyone who fights for civil rights and freedom of speech

CONTENTS

LIST OF CHARACTERS

Great Jacob - 7seven biological father

Dr.X - evil doctor that curse 7seven

Bc moon - old player 7seven met
in college

7seven

CHAPTER 1

COMING OF AGE 7

T HIS STORY IS ABOUT A kid from outer space named 7seven. He was born around 3,000 b.c on planet Saturn. He was the fastest, tallest dude in the first grade. Until he started playing football for the little league team New England Patriots. He ran a touchdown every play. No one could believe it. So they took me to play against a bigger, better team. They took me to another planet. We lost 42-6. But I was still an offensive genius just not that night. Then one day I went to the dental office to get a check -up. There I can in contact with the evil doctor x. the evil doctor threw a curse on 7seven. He knew 7seven was the son of a great basketball player named great Jacob. Doctor X said he curse seven because he was a racism and didn't like blacks.

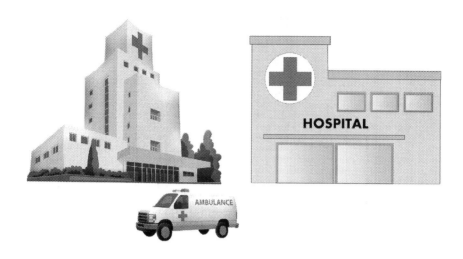

After the curse 7seven started to cry and became ill with sickness. He couldn't eat for days. Finally, his mom took him to the doctor but the good doctor said he couldn't work on him. So they took 7seven to a witch doctor, a preacher who haven't seen his daddy to see if he could help. The preacher took 7seven to a room where he prayed for him. But again the ritual did not help him. Finally, he started to feel better and regain his strength. He started to eat again. They told seven to keep what the preacher said to him a secret or else the curse would return and he be sick again.

EVER SINCE I WAS 7 SEVEN

CHAPTER 2

RETURNING TO SPORTS AFTER MY ILLNESS

REMEMBERING RETURNING TO SPORTS AFTER my illness. Even though I didn't talk much I heard a lunch lady say no more extra for u your no longer special. But any way back to sports. I continue to excel in sports even though I was overweight after the sickness. I excel in

football, baseball, soccer, track and field, and basketball. I excel in wr, qb, dl, lb and ol in football. I was especially fast and hand good hands at wr. We played at a high level. I know about good and bad coaches. I even had some bad coaches who told us not to do our school work and just worry about sports. Some guys did anything to get ahead for drugs to using the head to spear another player. But we was tough. I did my school work I wasn't growing up to be dumb. I had a big ego even in charlotte nc NBA all-stars games. Talking to mj parents and nephew for almost 2 hours so we could have met the players. It was fun.

EVER SINCE I WAS 7 SEVEN

CHAPTER 3

JR HIGH

M Y ILLNESS IS GETTING ME overweight. so I hope to become a pro football player. But the Junior high coach cut me twice back to back. I didn't give up

and fact I went straight home off the bus and starting playing basketball. I made the basketball team both years and starting to say I'm the next great basketball player. My head again gas. I had good 2 years in jr high basketball and dazzle the tri county crowd. But as I got older I started to think what's the real reason they cut me in football. Kind a strange for a big guy seem to be a sure shot in the pro's. Later in life I had to ask was it racism or what.

 **CHAPTER 4**

HIGH SCHOOL YEARS

B Y THE TIME HIGH SCHOOL year came around I had excelled in basketball a lot of places. From NBA star camp to acc camps. So the high school had already heard of me and some other guys and automatically place us on the squat. I average around 20 points and 1.0 rebounds a night. Even though sick still probably the most dominant player in 4a conference. Night after night I ruled the league. U couldn't tell the curse was growing on me. My DNA was dominant but Saturn didn't live up to her hype about what they claim to know. They claim to have dna specialist but now they lying and saying they can't

CHAPTER 5

MOVING IN WITH
MY STEPDAD

WE WAS MOVING TO ANOTHER city. My mom was getting married to my stepdad even though my told everybody he was my real daddy. When I first met

him he would say u not my child but because he was a recovering drunk I wouldn't listen or believe him. At first my parents had a violent relationship. Every weekend it would be gunfights. My sister said she had to move soon. And I quit sports because I was to overweigh and coaches work us like slaves. I quit and went to work at McDonald's and became an assistant manager. But deep down I still wanna to play basketball. So we out for the team my senior season at Saturn high. We were good but the coach cut me. He told me wait a semester u know me a ball boy and he try and play me in January. That was too much for me to over stand with situation in life and I had to quit and go back to work. My parents tough it out and stay together. I don't know why but I going to college an hbcu.

EVER SINCE I WAS 7 SEVEN

CHAPTER 6

GOING TO COLLEGE A HBCU

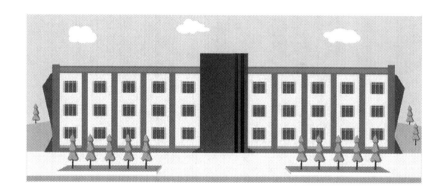

FINALLY, SEVEN GOES OFF TO college where he studied for around 300 years. He studies math, science, biology, chemistry and also studied plants used in medicine. Mentally his mind had suppressed all those things that happen in his earlier life. But while going to college he met a great space prayer by the name of BC Moon So the coaches started talking among themselves and about Seven great

career as a child. Even Seven's mind had heated up and he started to remember things also. Like the great curse doctor x had placed on him. Even though college bring about a lot of good things, it was also hard times especially trying to find a cure for the curse. Especially with no lawyer or experience on how to handle all this. But seven work hard and got a disability lawyer. Going to school was financially hard. With all racism and bias I could not handle all the pressure. Like matching DNA with great Jacob so I could get money from his estate. People would look Seven in the face and laugh. It was like the 60's all over again. Even with div.1a backing. He didn't Graduate. But he learned enough to come across the magic "space tablets" and regain his grip on basketball. The space tablets were 1Ox powerful.

CHAPTER 7

7SEVEN GOES TO JAIL AND CIVIL COURT

JUST LIKE ANY OTHER KID seven faces an unjust law system. Even though law and government is supposed to make society better but because of man and his faults

the system of law is broken. So one day while in college some police officers come and arrest seven. Even though seven didn't do anything wrong the cops still carry him away. They held seven in jail all day and night. They fed him poorly only bread and water. He called the guards several times but they only laugh at him. When seven ask what he was being arrested for the didn't answer. Finally, seven saw someone he knew for college a professor came to visit him. The professor brings good news that seven will be released very soon and has a basketball game to play. Finally, the guards release him and takes him to the gym to play his finally game because 7seven was black they denied him a lawyer for his civil cases. But before the game they took 7seven to civil court so he could use his lawyer and paralegal skills. So he could sue the government like any common sense individual.

EVER SINCE I WAS 7 SEVEN

 CHAPTER 8

SEVEN WINS A COLLEGE BASKETBALL CHAMPIONSHIP AND RETIRES

SEVEN PLAYED A GREAT GAME scoring over 50 points, 50 rebounds, 20 assists. The college he played for was named the hbcu champs. The crowd went wild. Although he never made it to the big league he still keeps his dream of playing in the big league alive. He had a couple talks with Saturn knicks but that was it. Finally, he came home to live a simple life. He never got married. He only had a dog as a friend. He stayed in the rural life where he went fishing everyday before he died at the age of 600 years old. Some people said he was the goat

Printed in the United States
by Baker & Taylor Publisher Services